NPL|F
Nashville Public Library | FOUNDATION

This book given
to the Nashville Public Library
through the generosity of the
**Dollar General
Literacy Foundation**

NPLF.ORG

LIGHTS OUT

Marsha Diane Arnold illustrated by Susan Reagan

Creative Editions

Special thanks to Cheryl Ann Bishop, former Communications Director of the International Dark-Sky Association, to Travis Longcore for referring me to *Ecological Consequences of Artificial Night Lighting*, to Paloma Plant of Fatal Light Awareness Program (FLAP) Canada, and to James Karl Fischer, Executive Director of the Zoological Lighting Institute.

AUTHOR'S NOTE

We hear a lot about air and water pollution but not as much about light pollution. Light pollution happens when there are too many—and the wrong kind of—artificial lights. Tall buildings with many lights confuse both migrating and local birds. Frogs don't sing under artificial lights. Fireflies use their glow to communicate, but they can't talk with each other when there's too much light. Nocturnal animals eat and hunt at night. If it's not dark enough, they can't hunt as effectively. Overexposure to artificial light changes the rhythms of animal and human bodies, sometimes affecting our sleep and overall health.

For centuries, people on Earth looked to the night sky for navigation, for inspiration, for wonder. But today, we can barely see that sky through all the artificial light. In fact, we see less than 1 percent of the night sky compared with people of the 1600s.

You can learn more about light pollution and what individuals can do about it through organizations such as the International Dark-Sky Association (IDA). Remember to observe International Dark-Sky Week each April. It's an annual event when stargazers around the world celebrate the dark.

Little Fox peeks out from her den.

Beetle flits above her.

"Lights out!" she barks.

But the lights stay on.

House lights
Car lights
Truck lights
Streetlights
Red lights
Yellow lights
Blue lights
Green lights
Floodlights
Boat lights
Searchlights
Bridge lights
Blinking lights
Flashing lights
Blazing lights
Flickering lights
Everywhere —
Lights!

Where is Darkness? Where is Night,
where coyotes sing, owls hunt, and
birds fly across continents,
where foxes move through the dark
and beetles are more than beetles?

Fox and Beetle wonder
if Night is only lost.
Out there. Somewhere.

And so, together, they set out.
Across the wide, wide world,
they search …
for the Dark of Night.

But everywhere – Lights!

High above them Songbird flies,

confused and ever circling.

Where are the stars to guide her?

Across the wide, wide world,

they search …

for the Dark of Night.

But everywhere – Lights!

In the wetlands, Frog quietly
waits to join a nighttime chorus.
Without Dark, only silence.

Across the wide, wide world,

they search …

for the Dark of Night.

But everywhere – Lights!

On the mountain, Bear is wakeful.

There's too much light to hibernate.

Bear bellows at the brightness.

Across the wide, wide world,

they search …

for the Dark of Night.

But everywhere – Lights!

Through the forests and the meadows,
across highlands, deserts, dunes,
on tundra, prairies, and high mountains,
they search.

They come upon a seashore.

Something's happening on the beach.

Baby turtles hatching.

Baby turtles scattering!

Fox and Bear run to the water,

Frog holding tight to Fox.

Swimming away from shore and lights,

they call out to the hatchlings to follow.

Beetle and Songbird call from above.

Now in deep water

the sky grows darker.

Beetle sparks … sparkles … glows.

More than a beetle.

Firefly!

The baby turtles follow Firefly and moon's glow.

Patterns of the Night emerge.

The hatchlings paddle safely away.

Fox and Firefly, Frog, Bear, and Songbird swim on

toward a dark and distant island,

And when they come to the darkest place of all

they can see …

Everything.

Shadowy shapes

Dappled gray

Silvery white

Shimmering bay

Mushrooms glowing

Fireflies

Moonlit garden

Shining eyes

Nighttime weavers

Webs of stars

Constellations

Venus, Mars

Great Bear, Little

Comet play

Dancing moonbeams

Milky Way

"Lights on."

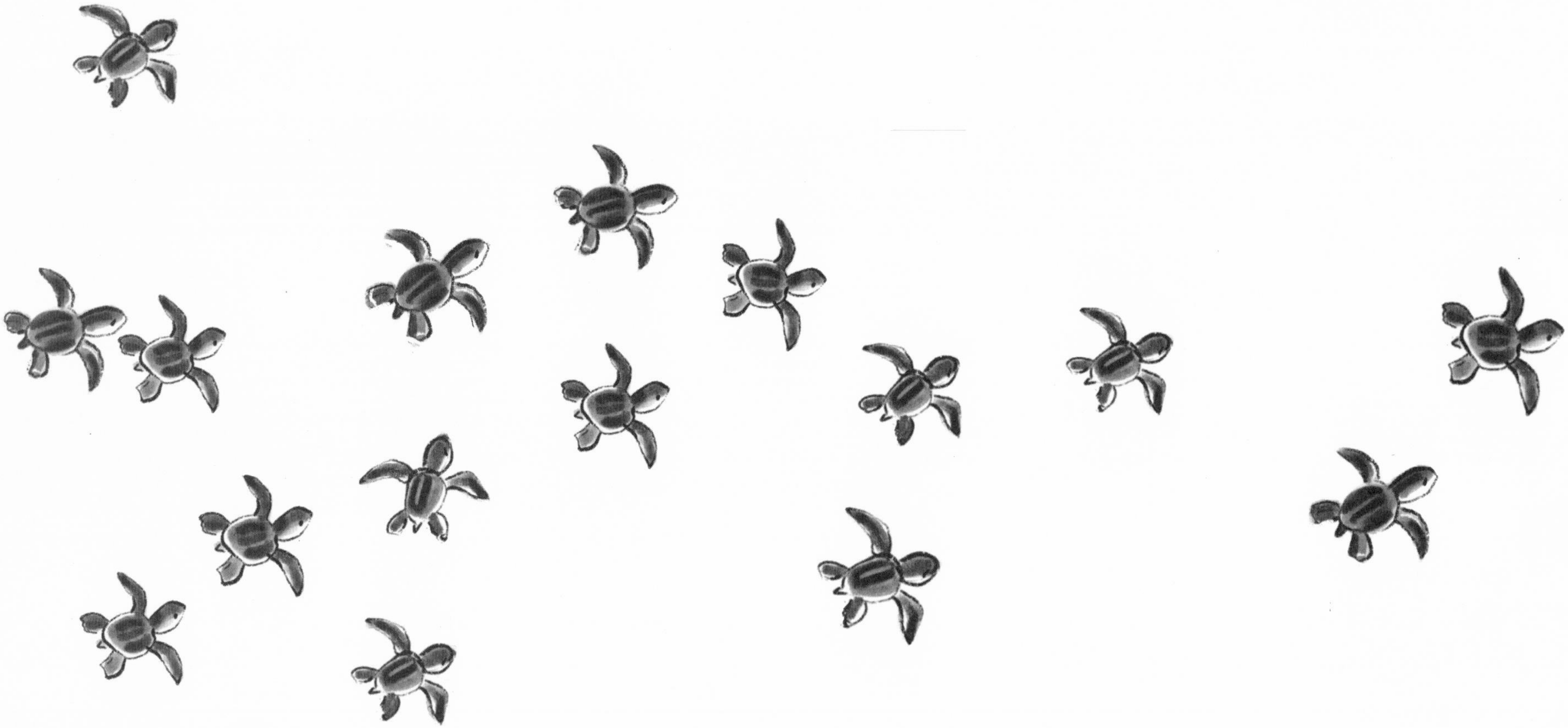